Flutternutter

Enjoy the
dance
of
our FL State
Butterfly!

The Dance of the Zebra Butterfly

Written by Deborah Burggraaf * Illustrated by Ronaldo Perez

Deborah Burggraaf   3-17-15   dburgg.com

ISBN 978-0-9892028-0-0

Library of Congress Catalog Control Number 2013936027

Published by
Protective Hands Communications
Riviera Beach, FL 33404
Toll free: 866-457-1203
www,protectivehands.com
info@protectivehands.com

Printed in the United States

Dedication

To Emily Drake and Ryan Alan Drake,
two beautiful butterflies in flight.

Deborah Burggraaf

To Wendy and Gabrielle
and
young readers everywhere.

Ronaldo Perez

Flutter me high,
flutter me low,
the Zebra's dance
is one to know.

I dance with striped wings,
soft yellow and black,
up high to start, then down low,
with a quick glance.

On blooms of blue Porterweed,
I pause and I rest,
only to see another Zebra Longwing
sipping nectar next to me.

Next, I flutter to sip nectar atop Firebush—
a real, sweet treat with golden dewdrops.
I soak up the Florida sun and do not rush!
So pretty to look at, but do not touch!

High on top of green leaves,
I flutter my black and yellow stripes;
a delicate dance of daylight dreams across
our painted white and blue sky—
Oh, what a sight!

Flutter me high,
flutter me low,
the Zebra's dance
is one to know.

On sculpted leaves of green,
I sit and I wait
for the moment to come,
when I lay my golden eggs.

Upon passion flower vines so green,
my yellow eggs are now laid.
Here I will molt and then change into
a black, spiked inching new queen.

I nourish on plants
and for two weeks, I molt and I change,
until I emerge a caterpillar, at first, all yellow!

Many would say,
"What a stunning, golden fellow!"

Flutter me high,
flutter me low,
the Zebra's dance
is one to know.

Several moltings have passed—
take a look; see me now!
I'm a stunning, black, dotted queen,
with bright spots on my golden crown!

For three weeks, I sit and I feed,
and now, I'm an inching, spiked caterpillar,
only a few can see.
Watch closely, as I will soon become
a rolled *Chrysalis,*
as if a curled up, crispy new leaf.

Now, as you sit and you wait,
soon you will really see,
not even a month has passed,
"It's me—it really is me!"

The wait is now over!
I spread my wings and flutter wide.
My yellow and black stripes
are nothing to hide.

On this special day, I emerge,
a *Zebra Longwing* you will now know.
Come and play with me today;
we have many places to go!

As we flutter in delight through pastures so green,
out to the canal—a wondrous sight to be seen!
The turtles and frogs sing a tune across the bay,
as we wave a, *'hello'* from our flight in midday.

The alligators are now asleep, basking in the blazing sun.
We flutter on by with our graceful dance—*oh, what fun!*
Past red Ibis and Blue Heron—a gift from nature we see,
as we slowly return to our roost in the tree.

As we settle in,
we must watch down below,
as the birds and the snakes
are keen to our flights—
that they already know.

Yes, the predators sit,
as we flutter to our roost.
Softly, we take our places,
on the leaves that we choose.

Flutter me high,
flutter me low,
the Zebra's dance
is one to know.

On bright flowers I feed,
searching for pollen with my tongue;
my long *Proboscis* now full of pollen,
as I flutter in the warmth of the sun.

Full of sugar
I sip the tasty delight;
but as darkness sets in,
I must return home from a day of flight.

To my roost of nearly fifty—
a treetop full of black stripes.
My familiar roost is a gathering each night—
"Oh, what a heavenly sight!"

The trees hold our soft capsules;
so tightly we are spun.
But now we must rest from the day that has passed,
fluttering across the hot, Florida sun.

One large family we roost,
in the high, leafy treetops.
We sleep into the warm night,
as the leaves whisper from atop.

Morning breaks a new day
and we unfold our soft wings.

Flutter by you;
flutter by me,
softly we dance in the breeze,
"Take a look—it's me!"
"It really is me!"

Slowly and gracefully,
we playfully sing,
as our black stripes softly beat
to the fluttering dance of Spring.

Flutter me high,
flutter me low,
the Zebra's dance
is one to know.

Again, we take flight
in search of purple Passiflora.
Today, it's our turn to lay new eggs
that will become butterflies tomorrow.

Our dance of slow grace—
a soft flutter in the breeze,
the tree limbs sway, too,
as we play in her leaves.

With only several months we have
to live life each day as we please—
each morning a charmed beauty;
each night a soft dream.

Flutter me high,
flutter me low,
the Zebra's dance
is one to know.

New eggs are now laid,
which again, will grow,
until the larvae one day,
becomes the black, spiked caterpillars,
that you *already* know.

On the leaves wet from afternoon showers,
and with lightning strikes from above,
I still flutter high atop the flowers,
as I watch the others now become.

Flutter me high,
flutter me low,
the Zebra's dance
is one to know.

"For my time has now come—
I must now return to the roost I call home.
I close my wings one more time,
as I watch from high above."

Once more, a spiked caterpillar inches out
and slowly crawls across the leaves, and soon,
new blossoms will slowly unfold
into a striped *Zebra Longwing*—
a budding, new bloom!

Flutter me high,
flutter me low,
the Zebra's dance
is one to know.

Come dance with me now,
as I take another flight!
For your eyes have beheld
a wondrous, earthly sight!

Of wonder!

Amazement!
A sight to behold!

A new Zebra Longwing has arrived
and now her story has been told.

Flutter me high,
flutter me low,
the Zebra's dance
is one you *now* know.

The End

Deborah Burggraaf was born in Danbury, Connecticut and later moved to southern California, where she lived for thirty years. In 2004, Deborah moved to Palm Beach County, Florida where she presently resides and teaches middle school.

Mrs. Burggraaf takes everyday wonders and unfolds them into inspirational stories for children. Her tales are often about obstacles and challenges to overcome, that in the end, make us stronger individuals. Deborah Burggraaf continues to encourage youngsters to follow their dreams each day.

Flutternutter is *Mrs. Burggraaf's* seventh book. Other titles include: *Caught in the Middle, Cooka, the Bird without Wings, Boonie—Freedom Runner, Crow No More, Hot Wheels for Benny* and *At the Pig Races*.

On her website: **dburgg.com**, you can download activities for each book, as well as contact the author, purchase books and schedule an appearance by **Mrs. Burggraaf**:

Website: www.dburgg.com · **Email:** deb@dburgg.com · **Phone:** 561-429-6733

Ronaldo Perez is an Educator and passionate lover of art and music since childhood. His mastery of the spectrum blossoms with every page turned in ***Flutternutter***. Mr. Perez's illustrations are inspired by the colors of nature and the vibrant rhythms of world culture, as well as those of his native, Haiti.

Flutternutter is Mr. Perez's first book of wondrous and original illustrations. Ronaldo's eloquent use of color and movement bring the Zebra Longwing to life.

Mr. Perez presently lives in Florida with his wife and daughter.

Email: ronaldoperez@att.net